Laughing Giraffe

HODDER CHILDREN'S BOOKS

First published in Great Britain in 2008 by Hodder Children's Books
This edition published in 2016 by Hodder and Stoughton

1 3 5 7 9 10 8 6 4 2

Text copyright © Bruce Hobson, 2008
Illustrations copyright © Adrienne Kennaway, 2008

ISBN 978 1 444 93600 1

Printed in China

Hodder Children's Books
An imprint of
Hachette Children's Group
Part of Hodder and Stoughton
Carmelite House
50 Victoria Embankment
London EC4Y 0DZ

An Hachette UK Company
www.hachette.co.uk

www.hachettechildrens.co.uk

Laughing Giraffe

Written by
Mwenye Hadithi

Illustrated by
Adrienne Kennaway

Hodder
Children's
Books

In the days long ago when Warthog was beautiful and Hippo lived only on the land, Giraffe was the noisiest animal on the Great African Plain.

He **SHOUTED** a lot and he laughed all the time.

In the Lucky Bean Tree, where the little weaver birds rested, Giraffe would

POP! his head up through the branches and take a mouthful of leaves and

HAW! HAW! HAW! with laughter.

The little weaver birds fell out of the tree with fright.

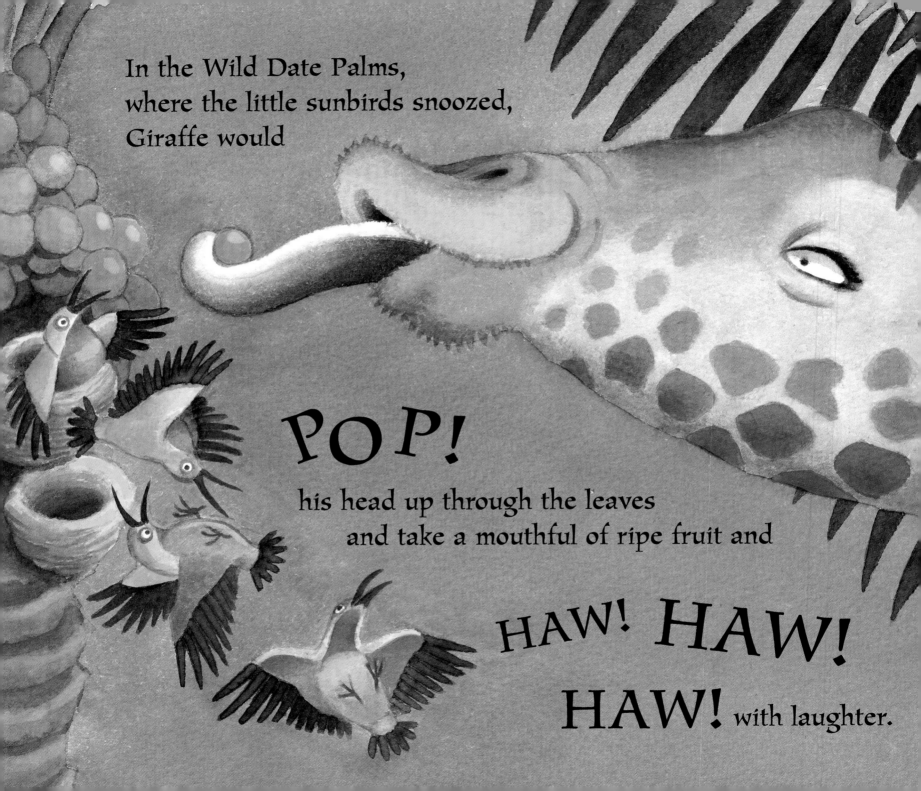

In the Wild Date Palms,
where the little sunbirds snoozed,
Giraffe would

POP!

his head up through the leaves
and take a mouthful of ripe fruit and

HAW! HAW!
HAW! with laughter.

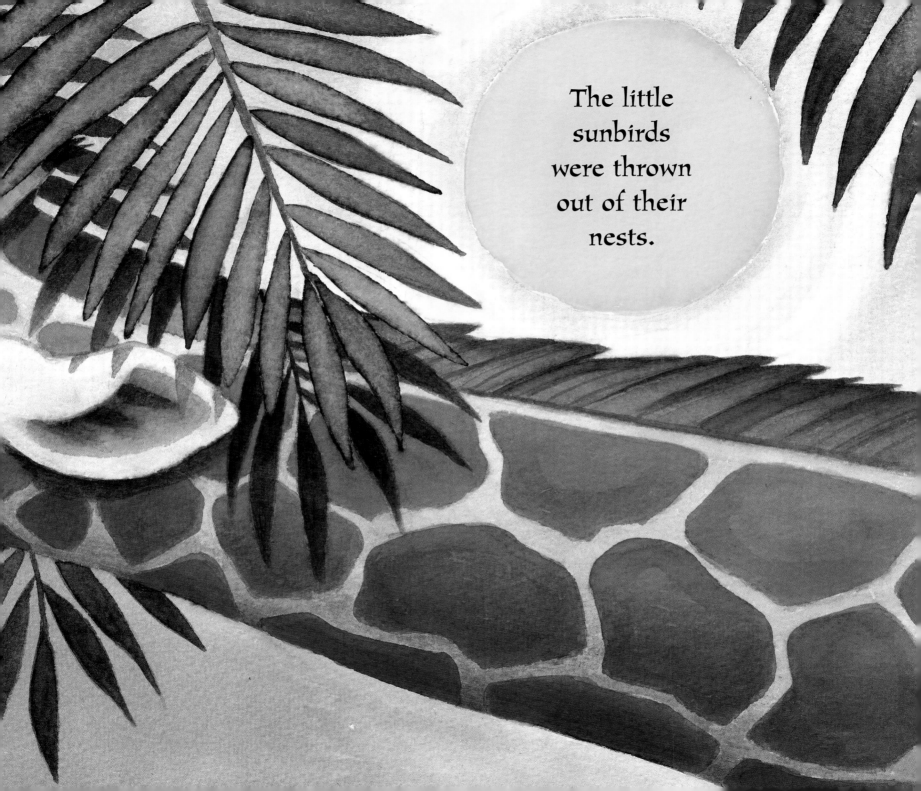

The little
sunbirds
were thrown
out of their
nests.

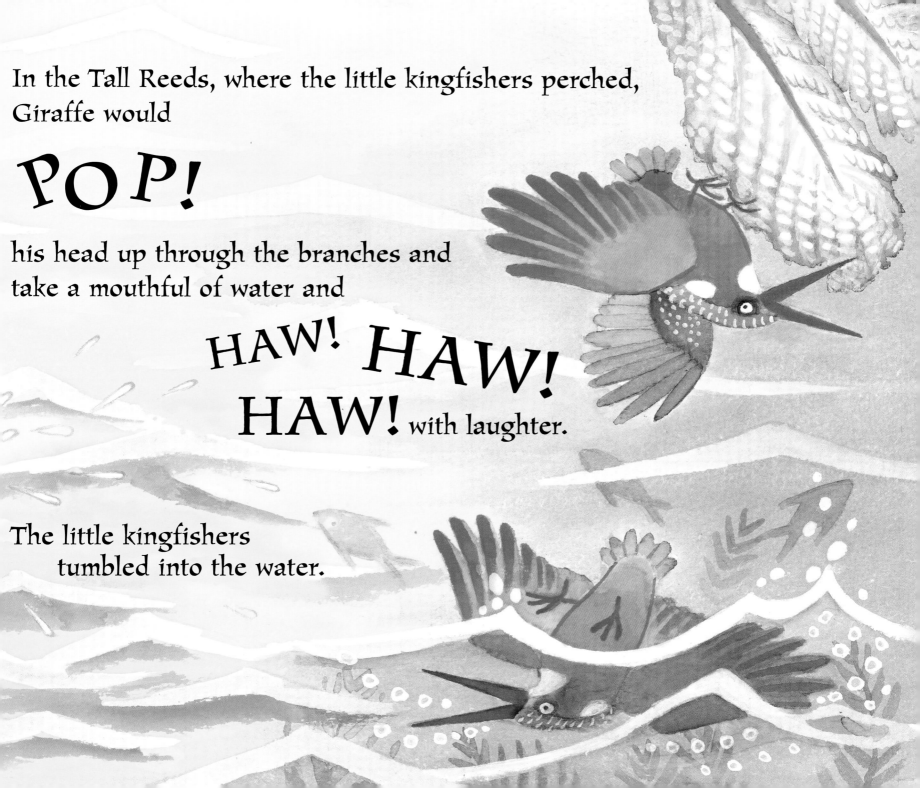

In the Tall Reeds, where the little kingfishers perched, Giraffe would

POP!

his head up through the branches and take a mouthful of water and

HAW! HAW! HAW! with laughter.

The little kingfishers tumbled into the water.

One day, when the little egrets were
sitting on a Toothbrush Bush, enjoying
the warm sun, Giraffe gave them such
a fright that the Littlest Egret
fell into a mud puddle.

"HAW!

HAW!

HAW!" laughed Giraffe.

"Giraffe!" the Littlest Egret scolded.
"You are loud and noisy and mean.
Anybody can be noisy all the time.
Even I could be as noisy as you if
I wanted to."

"You? That's a laugh,"
shouted Giraffe.

"Then we will have a
competition to see who
has the loudest voice,"
the Littlest Egret
challenged him.

"Agreed,"
laughed Giraffe.

"Then let us go
into the forest
and we will shout back
to the plain and see
who has the loudest voice,
said the Littlest Egret.

"And I shall judge the
competition,"
offered Kudu.

The sun was just above Giraffe's left knee
when they passed the Lucky Bean Tree
where the weavers rested.

The sun was just above Giraffe's neck when they passed under the Wild Date Palms where the sunbirds snoozed.

And it was just behind Giraffe's head when they finally stopped by the Tall Reeds where the little kingfishers were fishing.

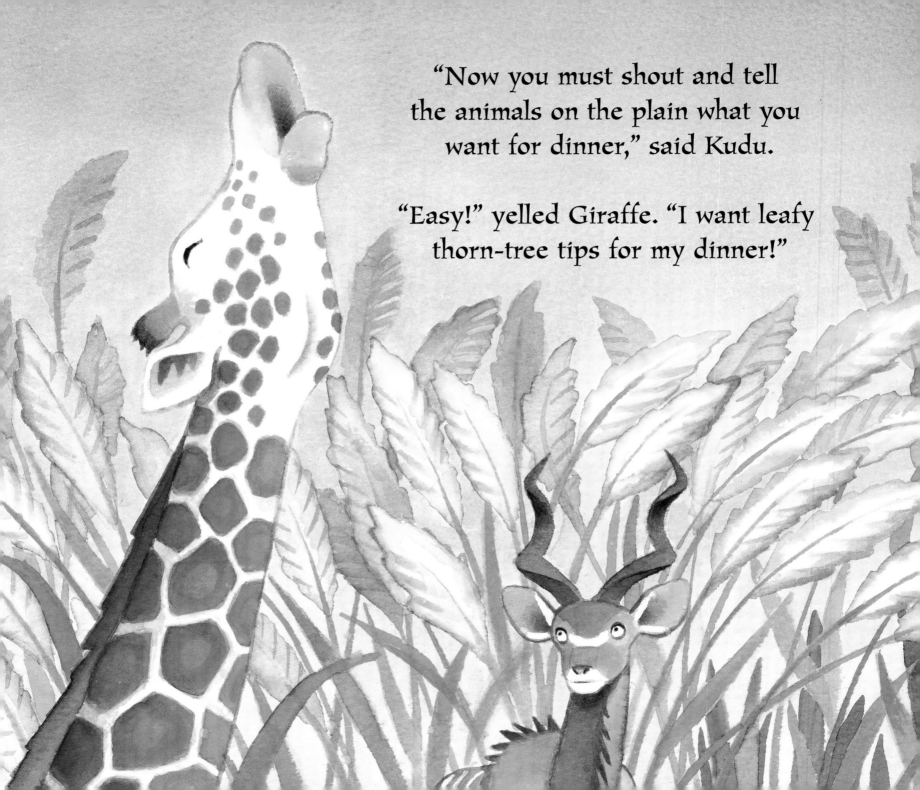

"Now you must shout and tell the animals on the plain what you want for dinner," said Kudu.

"Easy!" yelled Giraffe. "I want leafy thorn-tree tips for my dinner!"

And in a voice that could just be heard above
the breeze the Littlest Egret shouted,
"I want little brown beetles for my dinner!"

As they turned to head home,
the little kingfishers flew high in the
air singing, "Little brown beetles!"

As they passed the Wild Date Palms, the little sunbirds flitted from flower to flower singing, "Little brown beetles!"

And as they passed the Lucky Bean Tree, the little weavers were chattering, "Little brown beetles!"

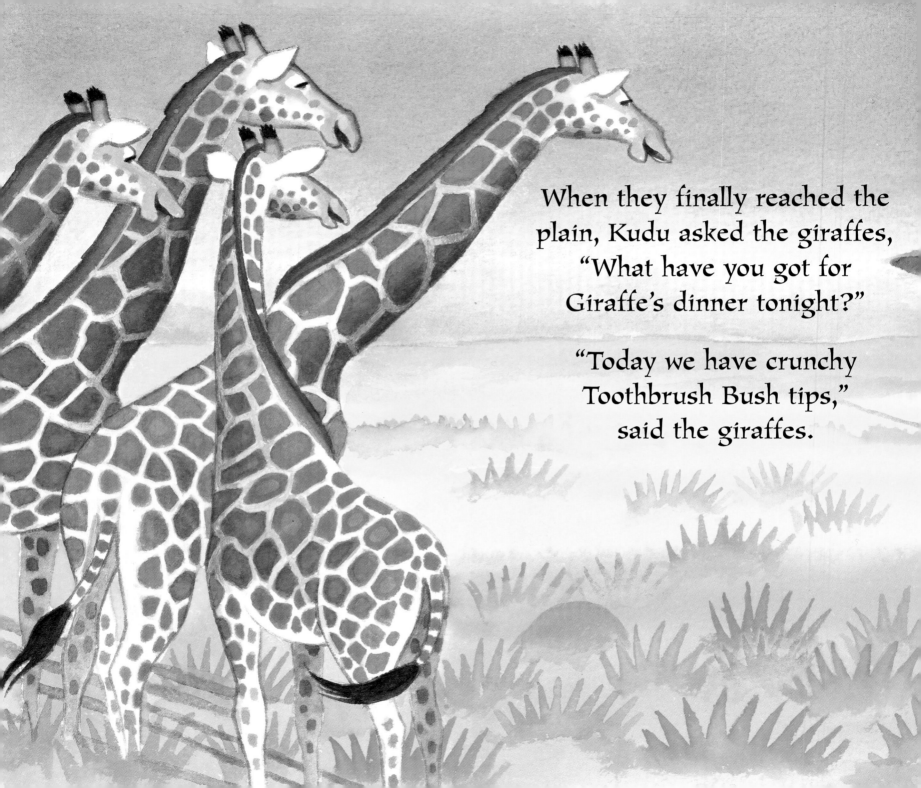

When they finally reached the plain, Kudu asked the giraffes, "What have you got for Giraffe's dinner tonight?"

"Today we have crunchy Toothbrush Bush tips," said the giraffes.

"But I wanted leafy Thorn-tree tips!" shouted Giraffe, crossly.

"Well, why didn't you say something?" said the giraffes.

Kudu then asked the egrets, "What have you got
for the Littlest Egret's dinner tonight?"

"Little brown beetles," said the egrets. "That is what she called for."

"Then the Littlest Egret has the loudest voice!"
said Kudu. "I declare she is the winner!"

The next day, wherever Giraffe went he heard all
the animals on the Great Plain whispering,
"The Littlest Egret has the loudest voice!"

And he stayed very silent.

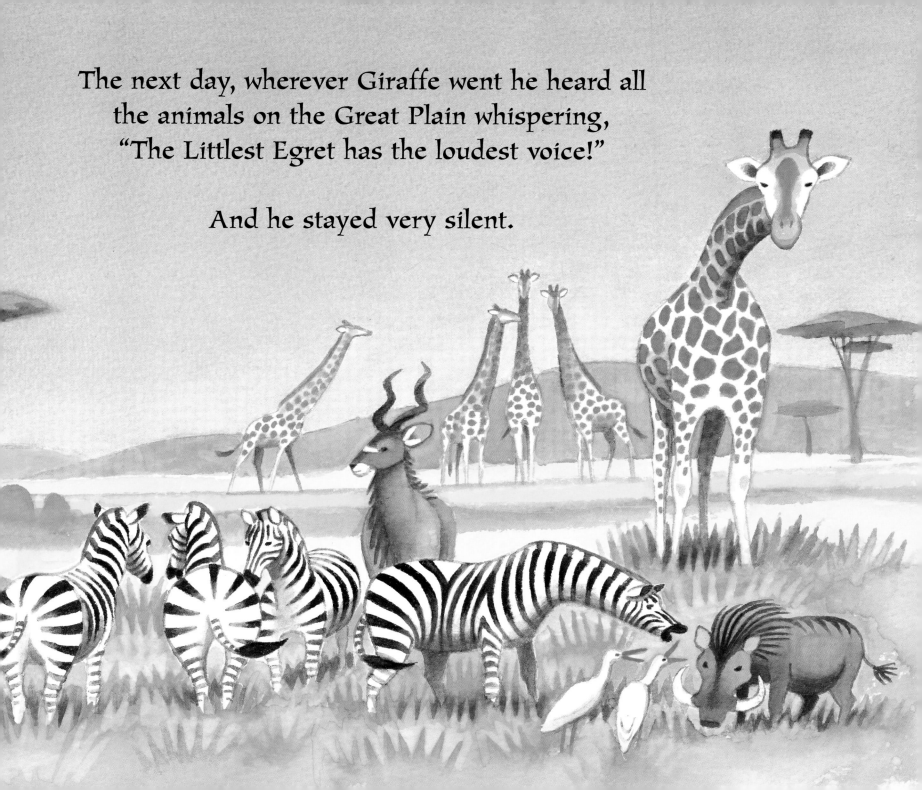

And so today Giraffe doesn't shout any more, and he certainly doesn't

HAW! HAW! HAW!

like he used to. He keeps quiet as quiet. But now and then Giraffe gives a little HRRRUMPH of a laugh and the other animals don't mind a bit.